TEN LITTLE
ANIMALS

Laura Jane Coats

Macmillan Publishing Company   New York

Collier Macmillan Publishers   London

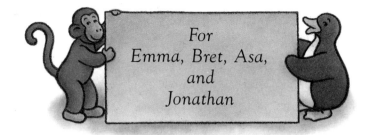

For
Emma, Bret, Asa,
and
Jonathan

Macmillan Publishing Company
866 Third Avenue, New York, NY 10022
Collier Macmillan Canada, Inc.
Printed and bound in Singapore
First American Edition

10   9   8   7   6   5   4   3   2   1

The text of this book is set in 19 point Goudy Old Style.
The illustrations are rendered in pencil and watercolor.

Library of Congress Cataloging-in-Publication Data
Coats, Laura Jane.   Ten little animals/
Laura Jane Coats. — 1st ed.   p.   cm.
Summary: A counting book in which one by one ten little
animals jump on the bed, only to fall off and bump their heads.
ISBN 0-02-719054-4
[1. Animals — Fiction. 2. Counting. 3. Stories in rhyme.]
I. Title. II. Title: 10 little animals.
PZ8.3.C59Te 1990   [E] — dc20   89-36778   CIP   AC

Ten little animals
Were sitting on the bed,
Waiting for a bedtime
Story to be read.

I climbed up to join them
And opened the book.
Then I thought I heard a noise
And raised my head to look.

10

Ten little animals were jumping on the bed.
The monkey bounced off and bumped his head.
I called the doctor, and the doctor said,
"No more monkeys jumping on the bed!"

Nine little animals were jumping on the bed.
The penguin bounced off and bumped his head.
I called the doctor, and the doctor said,
"No more penguins jumping on the bed!"

8

Eight little animals were jumping on the bed.
The hippo bounced off and bumped his head.
I called the doctor, and the doctor said,
"No more hippos jumping on the bed!"

7

Seven little animals were jumping on the bed.
The giraffe bounced off and bumped his head.
I called the doctor, and the doctor said,
"No more giraffes jumping on the bed!"

6

Six little animals were jumping on the bed.
The lion bounced off and bumped his head.
I called the doctor, and the doctor said,
"No more lions jumping on the bed!"

5

Five little animals were jumping on the bed.
The zebra bounced off and bumped his head.
I called the doctor, and the doctor said,
"No more zebras jumping on the bed!"

4

Four little animals were jumping on the bed.
The camel bounced off and bumped his head.
I called the doctor, and the doctor said,
"No more camels jumping on the bed!"

3

Three little animals were jumping on the bed.
The panda bounced off and bumped his head.
I called the doctor, and the doctor said,
"No more pandas jumping on the bed!"

2

Two little animals were jumping on the bed.
The elephant bounced off and bumped his head.
I called the doctor, and the doctor said,
"No more elephants jumping on the bed!"

1

One little animal was jumping on the bed.
The tiger bounced off and bumped his head.
I called the doctor, and the doctor said,
"Tell those animals it's time to go to bed!"

Ten little animals
Began to fall asleep.
I kissed each one
Softly on the cheek.

I pulled up the covers
And turned out the light.
"Good-night, little animals.
Good-night, good-night,
Good-night."

1 one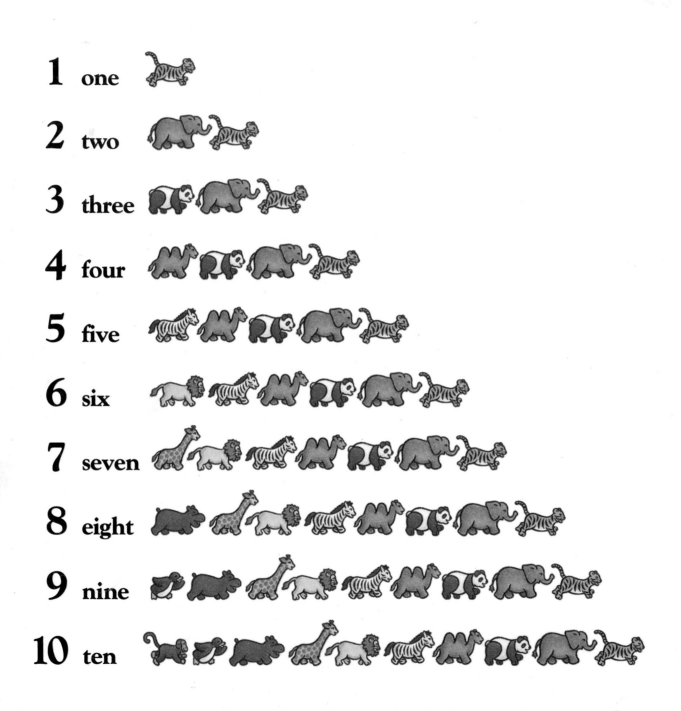

2 two

3 three

4 four

5 five

6 six

7 seven

8 eight

9 nine

10 ten